Pilgrim

A True Story

Written and Illustrated by Bobbi Schlosser

To Daniyel
Love, Bobbi
Fur Ever Friends,
Pilgrim & Lucy

Order this book online at www.trafford.com
or email orders@trafford.com

Most Trafford titles are also available at major online book retailers.

Printed in the United States of America.

ISBN: 978-1-4669-8968-9 (sc)
978-1-4669-8967-2 (e)

Library of Congress Control Number: 2013906586

Trafford rev. 04/10/2013

 www.trafford.com

North America & international
toll-free: 1 888 232 4444 (USA & Canada)
phone: 250 383 6864 ♦ fax: 812 355 4082

Dedication

To my beautiful grandchildren

The smallest kindness is never too small.

It was a cold, rainy morning just days before Thanksgiving.

The ladies were on their way to work when suddenly one said to the other, "Did you see that?"

"There was a cat back there on the side of the road with a can on its head!"

The lady that was driving the car turned around and went back to the side of the highway.

She stopped the car, got out and picked up the kitten. With some gentle twisting, the can popped off of his head.

"What are we going to do with him?" the one lady said to the other.

"We're going to take him to work with us!" said the driver.

They got a can of tuna and some milk from the kitchen area and the hungry kitten began to eat.

Soon, he fell asleep in the bed the lady made for him.

At the end of the day, the lady, who had taken the can off of his head, said, "Well, little guy, it's two days before Thanksgiving so I guess I'll call you Pilgrim. Would you like to go home with me?"

13

On the way home, the lady stopped at the store to buy some cat food and then she and Pilgrim headed straight for the bathtub.

The next morning, Pilgrim woke up to a cold nose in his ear. He heard a dog's voice say, "Who are you and what are you doing here?"

The kitten sneezed, and in a squeaky voice, said, "I think my name is Pilgrim and the lady brought me here. Who are you?"

"I'm Lucy and this happens to be my house! Why did she bring you here?" said the dog rather disgusted.

21

"I got lost and then I got hungry. I saw a soup can and I started eating what was in the bottom. My head got stuck inside and the lady came along and rescued me." said Pilgrim.

"My goodness!" said Lucy, "You are very lucky!"

"You have been given a good name because Thanksgiving is coming soon. The Pilgrims had a long hard trip coming to their new home, too. They came from far away and they were cold and hungry. Their Indian friends shared their homeland with them."

"I didn't know about the Pilgrims," said the kitten, "but I'm so thankful for my new home."

"I know you were here first, Lucy, but do you think we can be friends?"

Lucy looked at Pilgrim, nudged him gently and said, "Yes, I'm sure we can, Pilgrim. I'm sure we can."

The End

30

Bobbi is a Training Specialist at a facility for the disabled and operates the Art Department there. She is an accomplished artist in her area and has won numerous awards and is the past President of the Black Swamp Art Guild. She has seven Grandchildren and she and her husband Dave, along with Pilgrim and Lucy live in a cottage by the creek that you see in the book. She hopes that her message of caring extends to all that read "Pilgrim".

Edwards Brothers Malloy
Oxnard, CA USA
December 3, 2013